Kids love reading
Choose Yo

"The boo
the future

Katie Parker, age 10

"The adventures are really cool. Each adventure can be an adventure for you, but you are reading a book!"

Rebecca Frank, age 8

"These books are the best, everyone should read them."

McKenzie Tucker, age 11

"I love all the riddles, they are so fun! I did not know there were so many ways to go."

Charlotte Young, age 9

"*Choose Your Own Adventure*'s are full of adventure and mystery. You never know what's going to happen."

Benjamin Byrne, age 10

CHOOSE YOUR OWN ADVENTURE®

THE RESCUE OF THE UNICORN

BY DEBORAH LERME GOODMAN

ILLUSTRATED BY SUZANNE NUGENT
COVER ILLUSTRATED BY MARCO CANNELLA

CHOOSECO
WAITSFIELD, VERMONT

Book design: Stacey Boyd, Big Eyedea Visual Design

For information regarding permission, write to:

CHOOSECO
P.O. Box 46
Waitsfield, Vermont 05673
www.cyoa.com

Publisher's Cataloging-In-Publication Data
(Prepared by The Donohue Group, Inc.)

Names: Goodman, Deborah Lerme, 1956- author. | Nugent, Suzanne, illustrator. | Cannella, Marco, illustrator.
Title: The rescue of the unicorn / by Deborah Lerme Goodman ; illustrated by Suzanne Nugent ; cover illustrated by Marco Cannella.
Other Titles: Choose your own adventure.
Description: Waitsfield, Vermont : Chooseco, [2021] | Interest age level: 009-012. | Summary: "You make the journey across the ocean to Scotland, and vow to protect your unicorn from danger in these new, strange lands. Will the unicorn's magic reach those who need it most, or will it be stolen by the greedy and violent people who know its full power?"--Provided by publisher.
Identifiers: ISBN 9781937133672 | ISBN 1937133672
Subjects: LCSH: Unicorns--Juvenile fiction. | Magic--Juvenile fiction. | Rescues--Scotland--Juvenile fiction. | Unicorns--Fiction. | Magic--Fiction. | Rescues--Scotland--Fiction. | LCGFT: Fantasy fiction. | Action and adventure fiction. | Choose-your-own stories.
Classification: LCC PZ7.G61358 Re 2021 | DDC [Fic]--dc23

Published simultaneously in the United States and Canada

Printed in Canada

10 9 8 7 6 5 4 3 2 1

To my mother, a model of resilience and persistence

BEWARE and WARNING!

This book is different from other books.

You and YOU ALONE are in charge of what happens in this story.

There are dangers, choices, adventures, and consequences. YOU must use all of your numerous talents and much of your enormous intelligence. The wrong decision could end in disaster—even death. But don't despair. At any time, YOU can go back and make another choice, alter the path of your story, and change its result.

You have left your small village behind for new things. In the crowded port of Bruges, many chances for a new life await you. But when you stand before the giant ships, you see a caged unicorn. You know that's not right. Is the unicorn headed for a new life as well? YOU and YOU alone are capable of following this magical beast, and saving its life!

You knew your ride to Bruges wouldn't be luxurious, but it's not even comfortable. Each bump along the way jostles your spine. You are nestled between sacks of potatoes and carrots in a horse-drawn wagon headed for the city market.

As you ride, you clutch your unicorn-embroidered handkerchief. You think of your best friend Wiets about to sail off for adventure and opportunity. Meanwhile, you'll be left behind in Flanders. At least you can say goodbye and see him before he sails.

When you finally reach Bruges, all you can do is gaze at the towering belfry. It's twice as tall as any tree. Turning your head in another direction, you see the most enormous church you've ever seen! Not only that, there are hundreds of people, some of them speaking languages you can't understand. This place is so exciting that part of you feels like never going back home to your small village and tiny farm.

Turn to the next page.

2

It's market day, and you'd like to browse. Instead, you make your way to the docks where boats of all sizes line the waterfront. Bags, barrels, and boxes are being loaded onto the boats. You stop to watch some men struggle to load heavy rolls of woolen cloth. Suddenly, off to the right, you notice a crowd.

You wander over and squeeze through the people to find an iron-barred cage. There seems to be a small white horse inside. When you reach your hand through the bars to touch its flank, the animal turns its head toward you. You gasp with astonishment. It's not a horse; it's a unicorn!

Now, in 1510, it's been several years since anyone from your life in Flanders has seen a unicorn, and many people have started to wonder if any remain. Yet here is one, woefully caged, about to be carried onto a boat and away from Flanders. The unicorn slowly lowers its head toward you and its sky blue eyes meet your own. You shiver as a silvery tear fills the unicorn's eye and rolls down its cheek.

Your heart is pounding!

Turn to page 4.

4

"How dare anyone cage a unicorn! How dare they take it away from its home!" you say out loud.

"Watch out, you!" yells a burly man with a team behind him. Four men lift the cage and hoist it onto a ship.

Of course this isn't the first time you've seen a unicorn. It's been three years, but not only have you rescued an injured unicorn, you've even led a unicorn to your village to purify the well. With all the unicorn adventures you've had, you feel a deep responsibility to rescue the unicorn. But what about Wiets, waiting for you by the boat that will carry him off to sea? You really need to say goodbye to him!

If you decide to sneak aboard the ship, go on to the next page.

If you turn away sadly and try to find Wiets, turn to page 8.

You see a line of carts filled with cargo to be loaded. You slowly stroll past, until you spot a sack that's not completely full. When no one is looking, you scramble into the sack and find yourself surrounded by onions. Good thing you're small!

Before you know it, the sack is hoisted on board. "Careful with those onions, they're not rocks," you hear, and the sack is placed, not dropped, onto the deck. The onions feel scratchy against your face and you inhale bits of dust with every breath.

You don't dare wriggle around to find a more comfortable position because a moving sack of onions would certainly catch people's attention. Someone drags you below deck and you feel the rocking of the waves. You've never been on a boat before. It's frustrating not to see anything as you feel the boat begin to move forward.

Turn to the next page.

6

After what feels like months, but is probably only hours, you hear snores.

As quietly as you can, you wiggle out of the sack. The hold of the ship is almost as dark as the inside of the sack! You have to use your hands to feel your way past crates and barrels to reach the soft and silvery light.

Your hand touches an iron bar and you find the unicorn sleeping in its cage. The unicorn seems to glow like the moon.

Go on to the next page.

Reaching your hand into the cage, you gently stroke the unicorn's silvery mane. It sighs and flutters open its eyes. "I'll rescue you," you whisper, even though you have no idea how. The unicorn turns its eyes to meet yours and sighs again. You slowly slide your hand up the unicorn's horn, and the horn seems to glow more brightly with your touch. You are determined to save this unicorn!

You feel around the cage to find the door. Your hand touches a latch, but there's a large padlock on the cage door. Rescue is going to be more difficult than you expected! "Don't worry, I'll find the key before we reach land," you promise the unicorn. You reach through the bars to put your arm around the unicorn's neck and curl up beside the cage. You feel so content that you can't help drifting into sleep. Your dreams are full of unicorns.

You are abruptly awakened when a sailor shakes your shoulder and asks, "What are you doing here?"

Turn to page 21.

8

It takes a while, but you finally find your friend Wiets waiting impatiently several ships away.

"I was worried about you!" he exclaims. "My ship is almost ready to sail, and I would be so sad not to say goodbye!"

"Sorry to keep you waiting, but I just saw a unicorn being carried onto a ship!"

"A unicorn? I didn't think there were any left!"

A bell clangs loudly from the bow of the ship. "Better board the ship right now," a sailor calls as he rushes past.

"I made this for you," you say to Wiets, thrusting the unicorn-embroidered handkerchief into his hand.

Before he can respond, another passing sailor yanks Wiets by the shoulder, saying, "Let's go!" You watch him drag your best friend onto the boat. Suddenly, you are fighting back tears, wondering if you will ever see Wiets again.

And that reminds you—the unicorn! You might still be able to rescue the unicorn! You race back to where you saw the unicorn, but there is no cage in sight. You finally notice one ship is flying a unicorn flag, which seems like a good omen.

As you stand staring up at the ship with the unicorn flag, a smartly-dressed captain walks up to you.

Turn to page 12.

"Thank you, sir," you tell him. "I'm ready to go!"

The captain smiles and replies, "Call me Captain Hullett, and come, let me show you the ship."

Captain Hullett leads you below the main deck, past crates and baskets and barrels, and even a few chickens pecking at the wooden planks.

"Here you go," he says, pointing to a dozen hammocks swaying in the air. "Claim one for yourself. Stow your things below." He looks at you closely, maybe noticing your lack of luggage for the first time.

"Not traveling with much, are you? Come, I'll show you the galley."

You follow Captain Hullett toward the strangest kitchen you've ever seen. You are used to cooking on a hearth in your cottage, but this is just a pile of embers in an iron basin. Cooking utensils hang from the side of the ship. *Am I supposed to cook with seawater?* you wonder.

"You should begin preparing our evening meal right away," he tells you. "I'm going to start this voyage!"

"One thing, Captain," you call as he is already half-turned away. "Is there a unicorn on board?"

Turn to page 13.

"Looking for a job? We are about to leave, and our cook hasn't shown up." He points to the next boat over.

The captain reaches into his pocket and takes out a small drawstring bag. He plucks out three silver coins and holds up one. You see it is embossed with a unicorn head. "Three silver coins would be your pay for the voyage to Edinburgh."

But what about the ship with the unicorn flag?

If you choose to go with the captain on his ship, turn to page 11.

If you choose to sneak on board the ship with the unicorn flag, turn to page 14.

The captain throws back his head and laughs.

"No, the only animals we're carrying are those chickens, but if it's a unicorn you want to see, Scotland is the place. I've never seen any myself, but the Scots talk as if unicorns are as common as cats!"

Cooking for a dozen sailors and a few passengers keeps you busy from dawn until long past sunset. You collapse into your hammock each night and dream of a land where unicorns are as common as cats.

As the ship approaches Scotland, Captain Hullett calls you over. "You've done a fine job! I'd be happy for you to stay on and sail back to Bruges with us, but if it's a unicorn you're yearning to see, I'd recommend having a look around Scotland. Here, let me give you your wages."

He offers you three coins, not a fortune, certainly, but more than you've ever held in your hand at one time. Suddenly, your life seems full of opportunities!

If you decide to stay on board and return to Bruges with enough money to make some big changes, turn to page 24.

If you decide to disembark in Scotland to look for unicorns, turn to page 25.

When no one is looking, you scurry aboard the ship with the unicorn flag, and make your way down to the hold, the very bottom where cargo is stored. There's no one there, and it's very dark, so it's easy to hide.

Unfortunately, it is so jammed with barrels and crates that it's not easy to breathe. In the darkness, it's impossible to know how much time passes, but you sense it must be night when you no longer hear footsteps coming from the deck above. You are dying for some fresh air, and eager to get a glimpse of the sea.

As quietly as you can, you make your way up to the cargo deck, and to the main deck where you can finally breathe. The sea air is cool and invigorating. The moon is almost full, so you can see pretty easily.

You'd like to get a better look at the water around you, but the sides of the deck are high. You scramble up to stand unsteadily on the edge of the boat and gaze down at the inky waves.

Suddenly, a bell clangs loudly, startling you. Your body jerks, and you slip overboard!

Go on to the next page.

You splash around frantically, trying not to swallow water. If only you had learned how to swim! Despite your best efforts, you keep inhaling water, choking and coughing, so you can't even shout for help.

Your arm hits something, and you realize it is a piece of wood floating on the surface. You grab it desperately, gasping for air. You are too exhausted to do anything but catch your breath and hold on with as much strength as you can muster. You find yourself drifting away from the boat.

You float for hours, dazed and cold. You are surrounded by water and sky, nothing else, until suddenly . . . what is that? Far off on the horizon, there seems to be a boat. It is so far away you're not even sure it *is* a boat. Is it worth struggling toward something that may not even be a boat, or should you conserve your strength and wait for a better opportunity to appear?

If you start kicking toward what might be a boat, turn to the next page.

If you think you'd better save your strength for a more definite form of rescue, turn to page 19.

16

With every remaining bit of strength, you clutch the plank and kick toward the distant shape. Waves crash into your face and your eyes sting from the salt, but energy surges through your legs. That boat is your last hope!

Gradually, you approach the boat. When you are about 50 feet away, you see a smaller boat being lowered into the water. They're coming to rescue you!

Three sailors lift you onto the smaller boat and wrap a blanket around you. You can't stop shivering.

You climb a rope ladder up to the deck of the larger ship, where sailors gather around you. To your astonishment, someone calls your name! You look over to see Wiets pushing his way through. You hug.

"What happened to you?" asks Wiets. Your teeth are chattering too hard for you to answer. A freckle-faced sailor gives you a mug of hot water, and Wiets leads you below deck to a hammock.

Go on to the next page.

You climb into the hammock and realize you are utterly exhausted. You plunge into sleep to the strange rolling of the ship. Wiets stays by your side.

His face is the first thing you see the next morning. "Wiets," you say, "I want us to stay together, but I really need to find that unicorn!"

"That sounds like a great adventure to me!" he replies. "Let's talk to the crew for ideas."

You explain your quest to the first mate, Kees. He was the man who gave you hot water.

Kees thinks for a moment, then says, "I don't know about that exact unicorn, but I do know our ship is heading far to the north where the sea is full of unicorns."

Turn to the next page.

18

"The sea is full of unicorns?" You can't believe what you are hearing. You weren't even sure unicorns could swim.

"Absolutely!" he assures you. "I've seen them myself. On the other hand, when we reach Edinburgh, you might want to get off." He fishes a silver coin out of his pocket to show you the unicorn head on it. "If Scottish money has unicorns on it, I think they must be as common as cats."

If you and Wiets decide to stay on board to see the unicorns in the sea, turn to page 52.

If you two decide to get off in Edinburgh, turn to page 56.

You tell yourself that you made the right decision by waiting because as time passes, you can no longer even see what might have been a boat. It probably wasn't.

As the sun sinks toward the horizon, the sky blazes orange. It's as if the sea around you has turned to liquid fire. It's the first time you've ever seen such a sunset. For a while, you are so enchanted that you forget the danger that surrounds you.

Unfortunately, once the sun disappears, you're freezing. Your toes and fingers go completely numb. Water splashes into your mouth, but it's too salty to swallow. Your whole body shakes so fiercely that you can't even think. You fade in and out of consciousness until your arms slip from the wood and you slide beneath the waves.

Gradually you become aware that something is dragging you through the water. It's hard to see anything with salt water splashing into your eyes.

Turn to the next page.

Finally, you are pulled onto a sandy beach. An enormous gray seal flops beside you. You are relieved to be alive on land, but after hours in the water, you're freezing.

The seal barks, not unlike a fox, as it rolls from side to side. You watch in amazement as its belly opens and a human arm protrudes. Next you see a shoulder and a woman's head emerge. She climbs out of the sealskin, shaking wet hair away from her face.

It's a selkie! You've heard stories about seals that turn into women on land, but didn't think they were true!

"Thank you!" you exclaim. "Thank you for saving my life! I'm really grateful, but where are we?"

The selkie barks amiably and points behind you. There's a town, and with enormous relief, you see a yellow flag. You rub your eyes and look more closely. Yes! There's the black lion of Flanders on the flag! You haven't gone so far, after all!

Choking back tears of relief, you realize you've had enough adventure, and you never want to be on a boat again. You don't even care about that unicorn. You just want to go home. You wave goodbye to the selkie and start walking toward the town.

The End

"I'm here to rescue the unicorn," you reply.

The sailor laughs, slapping his thighs as if this is the funniest thing he's heard in a week. "You are, are you?"

You feel a bit embarrassed now, but take a deep breath. "Yes! A unicorn shouldn't be in a cage, and that unicorn shouldn't be taken from Flanders!"

He laughs again. "You know, this unicorn is going to have a very happy life in Scotland. You know perfectly well that there are hardly any unicorns in Flanders anymore, but in Scotland, people say they are as common as cats."

"If they are as common as cats," you ask, "why do they need our unicorn?"

"Well now, don't you think a Flemish unicorn is bound to be the best?"

You hadn't considered that.

"Seriously, from what I've been told, this unicorn is going to a great lord with a unicorn collection. It will be with others of its kind. It must have been very lonely by itself in Flanders, don't you think?"

That's another thing you hadn't considered.

Turn to the next page.

You spend the rest of the voyage contemplating the situation and learning a bit of Scottish from some of the sailors. To earn your keep, you mop the deck and clean the living quarters. You spend every free moment at the side of the unicorn. In fact, that's where you sleep.

One day, when you are cleaning the captain's quarters, you notice a beautifully inlaid box about the size of a loaf of bread. It looks like something a rich woman might keep jewelry in, but there's been no fancy dress on this voyage. You can't resist a peek! Inside, there is nothing but a silver key. Almost nothing is locked on the ship, not even the door to the captain's own room. You quickly pocket the key.

Go on to the next page.

That night, you slip the key into the lock on the unicorn's cage. With the slightest jiggle, the padlock slides open. You secure the lock again and return the key to your pocket. This could be useful.

"Don't worry," you whisper to the unicorn, "we're staying together no matter what."

As the ship approaches Edinburgh, you have to make a decision. It's true that the unicorn really might be happier with other unicorns, but on the other hand, it's a Flemish unicorn and belongs in Flanders. Who knows if it will enjoy being with a herd of Scottish unicorns?

If you decide to stay with the unicorn as it is brought to the castle, turn to page 33.

If you decide to rescue the unicorn now and try to take it back to Flanders, turn to page 38.

On the voyage back to Flanders, you think about your life there. With Wiets gone, your village will be rather boring, and taking care of a tiny farm all by yourself has been difficult. You're quite talented with a needle, but you have so little time to embroider because of all the plowing and planting you have to do.

When the ship returns to Bruges, Captain Hullett pays you three more coins. The six coins you hold represent your future!

You find an embroiderers guild in Bruges and ask to become an apprentice. Although you have to spend many hours with the needle, you still have time to explore the wonders of the city. You make friends with the other embroiderers.

Your hard work and talent are recognized and rewarded. Before long, you are promoted to journeyman, and then master. Your specialty is embroidering unicorns, and your trademark is a thin strand of silver thread flashing along the horn.

You never see a real unicorn again, but years later, you do run into Wiets, who is back in Bruges after traveling so far. Reunited at last, you two begin a *real* adventure.

The End

You wave goodbye to Captain Hullett and the crew. Edinburgh, where you've landed, is much smaller and much less grand than Bruges. You remind yourself that unicorns probably avoid big cities, so this may be for the best.

It takes you a few minutes to realize that people are talking, but you can't understand them. Even though you know a bit of Scottish, this is not going to be easy!

You wander a bit until a sign hanging over a doorway catches your eye. It shows a winged unicorn, something you've never seen before, or even imagined. You are just about to go inside when you hear Flemish being spoken nearby. Two young sailors are chatting in your language.

If you decide to go inside and see what the winged unicorn sign means, turn to the next page.

If you decide to ask the Flemish sailors for help, turn to page 29.

26

You swing open the door and step nervously into a shadowy room. It takes a few seconds for your eyes to adjust to the darkness, but then you notice a woman dressed in red. Her hair is red too, and it seems as if there are small stars tangled in her curls. She speaks to you, but not in a language you can understand. With an enticing smile, she beckons you to approach.

You take a deep breath to calm yourself and walk toward her. She takes your hands in hers, and this time when she speaks, you understand perfectly! She asks why you have come to Edinburgh.

"I've come to rescue a unicorn that was taken from Flanders," you explain, relieved that she seems to understand you.

Go on to the next page.

"Do you know it was taken here?" she asks.

"Not really. I just heard that Scotland is a place of unicorns, so I came to investigate."

The woman sighs and smiles. "Scotland is indeed a place of unicorns. Some people say they are as common as cats, but that's not exactly true."

At that moment, you notice a white cat brushing against the woman's ankles.

"Do you have winged unicorns here too?" you ask. "I saw one on your sign."

"Not yet," she admits. "They're called pegacorns. So far, they are more of a dream than a reality."

"Wow, I'd love to see one!" you exclaim.

Turn to the next page.

"In time, in time. But tell me, can you sew?"

"Actually, I've been praised for my embroidery," you answer with pride. You think about the unicorn you embroidered on the handkerchief for Wiets. *Where is Wiets now?* you wonder.

"I don't imagine you've done it before, but do you think you could sew feathers to make a wing?" asks the woman.

You shrug. "Probably."

"If you can do that, you have yourself a job here," says the red-haired woman.

If you accept the job offer, turn to page 70.

If you are determined to rescue the unicorn, turn to page 75.

You walk up to the Flemish sailors. "Do you know where I can find a unicorn?" you ask them.

"That's funny you should ask," one replies. "We delivered a unicorn just yesterday. It was on board all the way from Bruges."

You can't believe your luck! "Where is the unicorn now?"

The sailors shrug. "It was carted out of town yesterday," says one.

"They were taking it to a castle," the second sailor adds. "To the north, I think."

"Thanks!" you exclaim. "I'm off to find that unicorn!"

"That won't be easy," says the first sailor. "It's probably inside a castle by now, and there are many castles in Scotland."

"You'd have to go outside town, past the walls," says the first sailor. "When Flanders had unicorns, they never wandered around Bruges, did they?"

Turn to the next page.

You leave the walled part of town with little idea where you are headed. You use the sun to direct yourself north. You walk for hours through a narrow green valley between mountains.

The ground is spongy and with every step, water squishes around your feet. The earth in Flanders wasn't like this at all.

Your throat is parched, but after you've walked a long way, your ears finally catch the hushed roar of water rushing. The sound leads you to a dazzling blue pool of water fed by a waterfall, something you've never seen in Flanders!

Using your hands as a cup, you drink the sweetest water you have ever tasted. You splash some on your face, then soak your tired feet. Even though you don't know where you are, you haven't felt this relaxed since you left Bruges. Your eyes close and you drift off to sleep.

Turn to page 32.

32

When you wake, a strange and luminous creature is sitting beside you, stroking your hair. She isn't exactly blue, but there is a bluish light emanating from her. She sings to you, and weirdly, you understand that she's inviting you to join her in her home. You try singing your thanks, and she seems to understand. When you ask where, she points to a cave behind the waterfall. It's the home of fairies, she explains, and you are welcome.

If you agree to spend the night with the fairies, turn to page 130.

If you worry that fairies can be mischievous and you had better not trust her, turn to page 132.

When the boat reaches Edinburgh, you disembark, waving goodbye to the crew. You watch the caged unicorn as it is carried off the boat and lifted onto a horse-drawn wagon. The unicorn looks skittish, and you feel uneasy yourself, not knowing what will happen.

The wagon starts moving and you walk behind. Luckily, the wagon is going slowly so it's possible for you to keep up, but after a few hours, you are exhausted.

Turn to the next page.

34

By the time the wagon reaches a castle, you are weak with hunger, and your feet are aching.

Turn to page 36.

The arrival of the unicorn has caused so much excitement that no one pays any attention to you. You watch the unicorn being released from the cage, and you follow it to a large fenced paddock. You rub your eyes in astonishment.

There are at least ten unicorns prancing around. Their coats are almost radiant, and their horns are glowing. The Flemish unicorn is led into the paddock. You can see that it is in much worse health than these Scottish unicorns, but the sight of the other unicorns causes it to perk up.

You lean against the fence, watching the Flemish unicorn eat and drink until it is full. Then the unicorn comes over to you, and you stroke its mane consolingly. You feel so connected to this unicorn that you know you can't leave it.

The unicorns here seem to be taken care of very well, but unicorns are very independent creatures, and even in this comfortable life, you can tell they are prisoners. Your unicorn gives you another nervous look. Maybe you should watch and see more about what life here is like for the unicorns, or maybe you should free the Flemish unicorn right away.

If you want to stay on with these unicorns, turn to page 39.

If you want to help the Flemish unicorn escape, turn to page 41.

38

The boat docks. While the sailors are busy tying the ship and getting ready to unload it, you unlock the cage, jump on the unicorn's back, and gallop down the ramp. You hear outraged shouts behind you, but you don't even look. You nudge the unicorn's flanks with your heels and hold onto its mane as you race out of town into the countryside.

You know people will be looking for you, and it's only a matter of time before they will catch up to you. Not only that, the unicorn is panting. You can see that being locked in a cage during the voyage has taken a toll on its health.

You spot a barn up ahead, and you think about hiding in there for a while. On the other hand, maybe you should get off the road and go into the forest.

If you decide to see if the barn is a safe place to hide, turn to page 42.

If you head into the forest, turn to page 44.

The stable master notices you caressing the blue-eyed unicorn and says something to you, but you can't understand. He hands you a brush and gestures toward the unicorn's tangled mane. When the mane is clean and shining, you start brushing the unicorn's flanks. You braid its tail. By the time you're done, the unicorn looks a lot better, but still not as lustrous as the Scottish unicorns. The voyage was certainly hard on the poor unicorn.

When the stable master comes to inspect your work, he nods his head with approval and motions for you to follow him. In the stable, he shows you to a corner piled with hay. He hands you a blanket, a cup, and a bowl. It seems you have a job!

Turn to the next page.

40

Every day, you groom the Flemish unicorn first, and every day, it seems healthier than the day before. Its blue eyes shine and its coat becomes more radiant.

You take care of the other unicorns too, and before long it's easy for you to tell them apart. One has pale gray freckles on its nose, and another has silver streaks in its mane. Most of them have sparkling black eyes, but one is green eyed. There's an especially frisky little one, and another with an unusually pearly horn.

You don't know this, but all the workers at the castle start to call you "Little Unicorn" because they don't know your name. You spend so much time with the unicorns that sometimes you feel like you've become one yourself. It's the best job you ever could have imagined!

The End

You know you'll have to wait until night to try to free the Flemish unicorn, so you go to the stable and hide yourself in a pile of hay. Trying to ignore the gnawing pangs of hunger in your stomach, you do your best to nap. After several hours, you hear the unicorns being led in. You fall back asleep to the sound of twelve unicorns breathing.

The next sound that awakens you is the stable master's snoring. You hadn't guessed he would sleep in the stable too! Will it be possible to get the unicorn out without waking him or should you wait until he leaves, even though you won't have the cover of darkness?

If you decide to try to rescue the unicorn now, turn to page 59.

If you think it would be better to wait until daytime, when the unicorns will be outside, turn to page 61.

You slow down and climb off the unicorn. You peer into the barn. There is a lot of hay, but no sign of animals or people. As soon as you enter the barn, the unicorn starts munching on hay, and you wish you had something to eat.

You've only been inside for a few minutes when you hear someone whistling as they approach. You and the unicorn dive into a pile of hay and wait.

A boy enters the barn, whistling cheerfully. You can't see much, but you can tell that he is wearing what appears to be green moss. *Is that what people in Scotland wear?* you wonder. You watch him beckon toward the open door, and a flock of swallows swoops into the barn. They dart around the barn and finally settle among the rafters.

Meanwhile, the hay is making your nose itch. You try holding your breath, but it's no use. You sneeze!

Turn to page 48.

44

You lead the unicorn off the road and into the forest. There's no path, so you wander without direction. It's getting dark and you start feeling anxious. You need a protected place to sleep, and you're worried about the unicorn's health.

Just then, you come upon a strange creature lying on the ground. It's somewhat like a man, but larger, and has only one eye in the center of his forehead. Protruding from his chest is one hairy arm. He has only one leg. His one eye blinks and he smiles at you warmly. He waves you over.

Turn to page 46.

46

You feel really sorry for this creature and wonder how he even moves. Has he been enchanted by a terrible spell? You know unicorn horns can purify many things, and it seems very possible that the touch of the unicorn's horn might release this poor creature from a horrible fate.

Yet what if this giant is more dangerous than he looks?

If you decide to see if the touch of the unicorn horn can restore his humanity, turn to page 65.

If you think it is safer to leave this creature behind, turn to page 67.

You wait a few hours before leading the unicorn out of the barn. Even in the moonlight, it is hard to see. You're really tired, so you try riding the unicorn again, but slowly this time because no one is chasing you.

You are half-dozing on the unicorn's back when you hear a snarl. A wolf lunges toward you! The unicorn flings you off its back just seconds before the wolf attacks it. You are frozen with fear and horror. The unicorn tries desperately to shake the wolf off its side. Your heart seems to stop as you watch the wolf tear into the flank of the unicorn.

Without thinking, you turn and run while the wolf devours the unicorn. Did the unicorn sacrifice its life for you, or was it just instinct that made the unicorn throw you off its back? You're grateful and relieved to be alive, but heartsick that the unicorn is dead.

You walk back to Edinburgh, crying the whole way. All you want to do is go home and forget this ever happened.

The End

Your sneeze blows the hay away from your face entirely, and the boy looks right at you.

"Why are you hiding?" he asks in a calm voice.

You lead the unicorn out of the hay and tell him your whole story.

He listens, then says, "You must be hungry. Let me bring you some food."

The boy returns with some bread, cheese, and a flask of water. He sits down beside you while you eat.

"You must be very careful around here," he warns you. "Besides ordinary dangers like wolves, there are also kelpies, river spirits that turn into black horses and drown people. There's a one-eyed giant named Fachan, and an evil goblin called Redcap. You are welcome to stay in this barn tonight, and I can lead you to a safe path tomorrow."

You and the unicorn nestle back into the hay. As you are falling asleep you wonder—why did he speak to you in Flemish? How did he know you were Flemish before you told him? Is the boy magical himself? Protecting the unicorn matters above all else. What if the boy's magic can't be trusted?

*If you stay until morning,
go on to the next page.*

*If you decide to leave while it is
still dark, turn to page 47.*

It is easy to sleep.

When you wake up the next morning, the swallows are starting to sing. The boy is already in the barn, holding a piece of cheese.

"Good morning!" he says, brightly. "I have some food for you, but you'll need to go to the river for water."

"Sure!" you say. "I'm really thirsty, and the unicorn must be, too." The unicorn's blue eyes seem a little dull, and its coat has lost some luster.

"The river is just down that path," says the boy. "Here, take a bucket. When you get back, we can work out a plan for you to get back to Flanders."

You nibble the cheese as you lead the unicorn along a path through the pasture. The morning sun glistens on dewdrops. Sheep graze on the green grass.

As you approach the river, you see a girl about your age, splashing water onto her arms. You call out hello in Scottish, and she waves you over.

Turn to the next page.

50

You do your best to speak to her, but she doesn't say a word back. She just smiles at you as she continues playing in the water. Is it possible she's deaf?

You and the unicorn are both thirsty, so you crouch down to drink from the river. The girl has waded deeper in, and gestures for you to join her. The water isn't too cold, and feels great on your tired feet, so you do. Soon, the two of you are splashing each other and laughing while the unicorn stands on the bank, watching.

The girl gestures for you to climb on her back, and you do. She starts carrying you piggyback, and it's fun, but before you know it, she's going faster. You squeeze your eyes shut, and when you open them, you find you're not on the girl's back anymore—you're astride a black horse that's galloping deeper into the river!

You decide to jump off because this is getting scary, but you can't. Your legs seem to be glued to the horse's flanks. The water is deeper now, and the horse is swimming. The horse dives underwater, taking you with it. You can't breathe, and all you see is murky river water!

When your lungs are bursting, you open your mouth, and water rushes in. There's water all around you, no air to breathe. You thrash your arms, but your legs are stuck to the horse. Kelpie, you realize! This must be a kelpie!

That's your last thought. The unicorn waits on the riverbank.

The End

52

After a short stop in Scotland, the ship heads north toward Norway. The weather gets colder, and you don't see land for days.

One day, Kees shouts, "Unicorns! Come see the unicorns!" You and Wiets rush over to look into the water.

Turn to page 54.

54

You see horns, sure enough, but they aren't unicorn horns. For one thing, they are dark, and the animal the horn protrudes from definitely isn't a unicorn. It's more like a giant seal. You've never seen a whale, but you've heard about them, and it occurs to you that this could be a whale.

"Those aren't unicorns," you tell Kees, and Wiets nods his head in agreement.

"Sure they are," says Kees. "Look at the horns!"

"It takes more than a horn to make a unicorn, Kees," you insist. "Unicorns are like small horses, and these are like big fish."

You are about to continue when Kees grabs your shoulder and turns you around. There you see the most gigantic creature emerging from the waves!

Turn to page 89.

You take a deep breath and step into the stone circle. At first, the drumming sound is deafening, but it soon changes to thunder. You watch lightning split the sky. Just as you are wondering why there isn't any rain, a bolt of electricity races from the sky to the top of your head, down your spine, through your legs, and into the earth!

With one quick sizzle, you've left this world.

The End

56

When the ship reaches Edinburgh, you and Wiets say goodbye to the crew. To your disappointment, Edinburgh is much smaller than Bruges. There is no tall belfry or beautiful church. What's more, you can't understand the language!

"This is going to be much harder than I thought," Wiets says.

As you nod in agreement, you get an idea. "Give me that handkerchief I made for you!"

You unfold the handkerchief to show the carefully embroidered unicorn, then approach the first person you see. You show her the unicorn and ask, "Where?" It's one of the very few words you know in Scottish.

Unfortunately, you don't know any of the words in her answer!

You point to the north, then to the east, south, and west. The woman understands, and points to the west. You thank her and head in that direction.

Go on to the next page.

"Where are we going?" asks Wiets.

"I don't know. Let's just keep an eye out for a unicorn."

You leave the walled part of the city and continue west. The landscape is very different from Flanders. There are rocky hills and the ground is boggy with lots of mud and puddles. You see sheep grazing, but no unicorns. Each time you come across a person, you show the embroidered unicorn and ask where.

You've been walking for hours when Wiets says, "Is that a castle over there? Anyone who could bring a unicorn from Flanders must be rich, so maybe that's where the unicorn is."

"At the very least, maybe we could sleep there," you add.

Turn to the next page.

58

You haven't even stepped beyond the castle walls when you hear loud laughter, shouting, and every now and then, something that might be music. You and Wiets look at each other uneasily, but continue inside. The courtyard of the castle is filled with people. Some are singing, others are throwing things in some kind of contest, and a lot are just yelling and drinking ale.

A big man says something to Wiets. Confused, Wiets tries to repeat what the man said, but that seems to infuriate the man. Wiets tries again, and the man gets even angrier. He punches Wiets in the face, knocking him down! Then another man jumps on Wiets and starts hitting him!

If you immediately try to pull the man off Wiets and stop the fight, turn to page 105

If you run to get help, turn to page 106.

You decide you must take your chances right now to rescue the unicorn. As quietly as you can, you push your way out of the pile of hay and unlatch the nearest stall. It's too dark to check the eye color of the unicorns, but you know the Scottish ones are all in much better shape. You quietly enter each stall until you find the one unicorn with a rougher coat and matted mane.

The unicorn is sleeping—something else you hadn't counted on—so first you have to gently wake it up. You stroke its mane and whisper in its ear, "Get up, get up! You're going to be free!"

The unicorn slowly blinks its eyes open, snorts, and closes them again.

Turn to the next page.

"Unicorn, it's me," you whisper. This unicorn seems to recognize your voice. It opens its eyes and lifts its head. "Come, let's go."

You guide the unicorn past the other stalls, and hold your breath as you pass the sleeping stable master. The stable door is bolted shut. As you slide it open, it squeaks.

The stable master immediately sits up, looks around, and sees you. Before you can even get the door open, he's grabbed you and is furiously shouting.

You end up in the castle dungeon! Stealing a unicorn, especially a blue-eyed one imported from Flanders, is a very serious crime. You never see a unicorn again. In fact, you never see daylight again.

The End

You return to the pile of hay. You try to go back to sleep, but all you can think about are ways to free the unicorns.

You remain hidden when the stable master awakes. He and three stable boys lead the unicorns out of their stalls and back into the fenced paddock. You hear them cleaning out the stalls.

After a while—you have no idea how long, but it feels like forever—you hear a bell ringing, and the stable boys and master abruptly leave the area. Now is your chance!

You scramble out of the hay pile, run out of the stable, and fling open the gate to the paddock where the unicorns are grazing.

Nothing happens. They don't even look up from the grass.

Turn to page 64.

The unicorn is not even breathing heavily when you hear the thunder of hooves. Turning, you see a pack of running dogs followed by dozens of men on horses galloping up the path behind you. You know you can't outrun them.

Still galloping, you look around. There's a river to your right. You can't swim, but maybe the unicorn can.

To your surprise, the unicorn doesn't cross the river, but rather continues galloping in it because the water isn't that deep. Water splashes all around you. The wet mane is slippery, and it's all you can to do to continue holding on. When you look up, your heart stops.

The river is flowing into a waterfall!

Turn to page 125.

64

You look for the blue-eyed unicorn and climb on its back. "Come on," you say, digging your heels into its flanks. "Let's go!"

As you ride toward the gate, the other unicorns lift their heads to watch. A few animals amble over and follow you. You beckon the others. They are much more relaxed about their escape than you would like, but there's nothing you can do about it. You can't rescue all of them, so what happens next will depend on what the unicorns choose to do. At least if they are outside of the paddock, they will cause a distraction.

Finally, when all the unicorns are wandering freely outside the paddock, you grab the unicorn's mane and slap its neck lightly while squeezing your heels into its flanks. It's time to gallop!

Turn to page 63.

With a heart full of compassion, you guide the unicorn's head so its horn can touch the one-eyed giant. You can feel the unicorn is shaking, and its eyes bulge with panic. The tip of the unicorn horn barely grazes the one-eyed monster's head before the unicorn flings its head back.

Nothing happens, except the unicorn is stepping away. The giant crawls toward you, and now you know you've got to get away!

You quickly lead the unicorn away from the one-eyed giant. The two of you hurry through the forest for a while before the trees dwindle, and you are back in the open air. The sun is just rising, and even though you're tired, you admire the rosy light of the vast sky. The earth around you is a lush green, but the ground is boggy and water oozes around your feet.

Turn to the next page.

The sun is halfway up the sky when suddenly, the unicorn's ears twitch and it pauses. Then the unicorn starts galloping forward! You have no idea what's happening, but you have to run to catch up.

Then you see it in the distance—a herd of about a dozen unicorns grazing in a meadow!

The unicorn races to them, and you dismount. The unicorns caress their heads against each other, and you could swear the unicorn is smiling. Its horn is starting to glow. The unicorns all ignore you.

You have never seen the Flemish unicorn this happy. As much as you want to bring the unicorn back to Flanders, you can tell that it is delighted to be with the others. Maybe it belongs here with the Scottish unicorns, not alone in Flanders.

You wave goodbye to the unicorn, but it doesn't even notice. You're heading back to the harbor so you can find a way back to Flanders where you, after all, *do* belong.

The End

You start to walk away when the monster suddenly wraps its one arm around your ankle and drags you toward it. More quickly than you can imagine, the giant twists himself around you. In a matter of minutes, you are gasping because you can't expand your lungs to breathe. You start seeing spots, but between the spots, you see the unicorn's head coming closer.

Everything is black. You feel something—the unicorn's horn?—gently touch your forehead.

Turn to the next page.

68

When you open your eyes, the first thing you notice is that you can breathe! You scramble to your feet and immediately notice you have four of them! You look down and see four white legs with hooves. You shake your head with disbelief and feel the weight of something protruding from the top of your head. You try to move your hands to feel what it is, but you don't have arms anymore.

What?

The unicorn moves toward you and caresses your head with its own. The unicorns's four legs look exactly like your four legs.

"It's going to be all right," the unicorn tells you. "I'll teach you how to be a unicorn. Now let's go."

Without even looking at the giant, the two of you prance through the forest.

The End

"Thank you!" you reply. "When can I start?"

"Right after we are properly introduced! You may call me Dame Scotia."

You introduce yourself and follow Dame Scotia into another room where two more white cats are sunning themselves in a patch of light near the window. She shows you a large wing partially covered with white feathers, but it's not like any wing you've ever seen on a bird. For one thing, it's as large as your outstretched arms. It doesn't appear to have ever been part of a bird. Is it for a costume?

Dame Scotia hands you a basket of white feathers, then pulls a needle and thread out of her pocket. "Why don't you continue sewing feathers on the wing while I prepare some tea for us?"

Sewing feathers is pretty tricky work. Another white cat appears and sits at your feet, purring. As you sew, you wonder where you will sleep that night.

As if she's read your thoughts, Dame Scotia appears with a cup of tea for you and explains, "Your food and lodging are included in this job. There's a nice cozy room for you upstairs." She examines your sewing and smiles. "Excellent work!"

You've finished one wing by the end of the day and sew another the next day. On your third day there, Dame Scotia announces, "We're ready to create a pegacorn!"

Turn to page 72.

72

She picks up one of the white cats, puts it in the center of the floor, and strokes its back until it falls asleep. You watch Dame Scotia arrange the two wings on either side of the cat. She combs her fingers through her red hair, picking out a few small stars. She sprinkles the stars over the sleeping cat. Closing her eyes, she murmurs words you can't understand.

In a matter of minutes, the cat has transformed into a winged unicorn! You rub your eyes with disbelief, and suddenly understand that Dame Scotia is no ordinary woman. "You turned a cat into a unicorn?"

Dame Scotia smiles. "That's why we say unicorns are as common as cats here. Pegacorns, however, are my new creation. In fact, this is my first. Now let's see how those wings work."

Turn page 74.

74

She strokes the pegacorn's head and it scrambles up, calmly looking around. With her hand on its back, Dame Scotia leads the pegacorn outdoors.

"If I get a bridle, would you ride the pegacorn into the air?" she asks you.

This is the most exciting offer you have ever had! While Dame Scotia puts the bridle on the pegacorn, you climb on its back. Taking the reins, you ask, "What do I do to make it fly?"

The words have barely left your lips when the pegacorn saunters, and the silverly wings start to flap. Great swooshes of air pass you. You feel yourself rising and squeeze your legs around the pegacorn's body. You're flying!

You circle around Dame Scotia's house and notice you can see the harbor. You make larger and larger circles until you are flying over the water. Suddenly, it occurs to you that you might be able to fly back to Flanders.

If you decide to fly back home, turn to page 77.

If you decide to return to Dame Scotia, turn to page 79.

"Thanks," you say, "but I've got unicorns to find."

The red-haired woman sighs. "You're going to need help. Here, take one of my cats."

She picks up the cat and places it in your arms. Almost immediately, it blinks its green eyes and begins purring. You've always liked cats, but having one now seems like it will just complicate travel.

"I can't take your cat," you say. "I don't think I will be able to take care of it on my journey. Besides, a cat might scare off a unicorn."

The woman smiles with secret amusement that you don't really understand. "It's up to you, of course, but Eleanor would make an excellent companion."

If you return the cat to the woman, turn to page 80.

If you accept the cat, turn to page 84.

You feel a little bad about stealing the pegacorn, but you're certain that Dame Scotia will be able to make another. Besides, you can't wait to introduce the pegacorn to Flanders!

You get your bearings by using the position of the sun to figure out which direction is south, and turn the pegacorn's head toward Flanders. It does occur to you that this journey could take several days, but you have time.

It's true you failed to return the unicorn to Flanders, but you introduce a pegacorn that turns out to be the sensation of the nation! You are famous, you're happy, and you have a pegacorn that loves you!

The End

You circle back to Dame Scotia, who is waiting in the yard behind her house. You really aren't sure how to make the pegacorn land, but you press your hand on its neck, directing its head downward. The pegacorn gradually slows and, with a few skips, lands in the yard.

Your heart is pounding! Dame Scotia hugs you and says, "We're a team! Let's give this pegacorn something to eat and then get started on another! I want this pegacorn to have a friend of its own kind."

Every week, you and Dame Scotia create another pegacorn, and almost every day you fly.

The End

"That's very generous of you," you say, "but I really can't travel with a cat."

"Be very careful of Redcap," she warns, but you are already waving goodbye.

It's a bit of a shock to return to the streets filled with people speaking an unfamiliar language, but you communicate your desire to buy some food. The coins you earned on board the ship are welcomed by shopkeepers.

Go on to the next page.

You head out of town, not really knowing where you are going. You think back to the woman's warning about "Redcap," and pay attention to what people are wearing on their heads so you don't run into trouble. It occurs to you that she was wearing red too, and you try to remember if she had a cap herself. You only remember the stars in her hair.

Turn to the next page.

82

You walk for hours, and it's getting dark. Not too far away, you see what might be the ruins of an ancient castle. It seems a bit spooky, but at least you wouldn't have to sleep in the open, so you step off the path and head to the castle.

The castle must have been grand once, but now the roof has caved in, and one whole wall has collapsed. Vines grow over much of the remains. Still, it's better than sleeping out in the open, so you walk inside, stepping carefully over fallen stones.

You are squatting in what might once have been a grand hallway, eating the food you bought in town, when you hear a strange rhythmic clanking sound. It's as if someone wearing heavy iron boots is approaching.

A chill runs up your spine. Maybe the castle is haunted!

If you decide to run out of the castle as fast as you can, turn to page 94.

If you decide to hurry up a staircase, turn to page 96.

"Well, thank you," you say, still feeling skeptical. "Do I have to carry Eleanor the whole time or will she follow me?"

"Just the opposite," says the woman. "I suggest *you* follow Eleanor."

You put Eleanor on the ground and she walks out the door, flicking her tail. You turn to follow, waving goodbye to the woman with red hair.

Following a cat through the streets of town might be the most ridiculous thing you've ever done, but no one seems to pay any attention to you. You walk through an opening in the walls that surround the town, and follow Eleanor down a winding path into the wilderness.

The land looks nothing like Flanders. It's much hillier, and in the distance, you can even see mountains. The ground is soggy, and water often oozes around your feet.

You reach a strange circle of tall stones that's like nothing you have ever seen before. You pause, tempted to explore them, but Eleanor prances ahead, her tail bobbing in the air. She leads you to a small stone cottage with a mossy roof.

The door swings open before you even knock. A white-haired man comes to the door, takes one look at the cat, and exclaims, "Eleanor! What a wonderful surprise!" He cradles the cat in his arms.

Turn to the next page.

"How do you know Eleanor?" you ask.

"She's one of my sisters," he replies.

"You mean one of your sister's cats?" you ask him.

"No, one of *my* sisters."

You look at him carefully and notice he does have strange catlike ears. In fact, his mustache is really a lot more like whiskers than any mustache you've seen before. He beckons you in, and when he turns, you notice a long white tail protruding from his tunic.

You're really curious about his tail, but instead ask, "How did you know I speak Flemish?"

"Oh, is that what your language is called? I just speak what I need to."

He looks at you closely, gazing directly into your eyes. "Don't do it," he says.

"Do what?"

"You want to explore the stone circle nearby, but don't. It's not a place for you."

"I won't," you say, but the truth is, you are more eager than ever to have a closer look.

He looks at you again and sighs. "Let me give you and Eleanor something to eat, and then the two of you can sleep by my fire. It's getting too late for you to continue your journey."

He serves you and Eleanor each a small fish and a bowl of milk. You don't remember seeing any water or cows nearby. *Where did the food come from?* you wonder.

Turn to page 88.

While you are eating, he makes a nest of blankets for you by the hearth. "I think you'll be comfortable here," he says. "Good night."

You crawl under the blankets and Eleanor nestles beside you. You try to sleep, but too many questions are racing through your mind. Is he a man or a cat? And what about Eleanor? Is she really just a cat? What about that stone circle? Why shouldn't you go there? As you puzzle over these mysteries, you become aware of the faint sound of drums.

It must be raining, you think to yourself. You snuggle deeper into the blankets and Eleanor licks your cheek. The more you listen, the more certain you are that you are hearing drums, not rain.

You scramble out of bed, wrapping one of the blankets around you. As you open the door, Eleanor meows. Her tail is standing straight up in the air. You ignore her, and shut the door behind you.

There is just enough moonlight for you to see the stone circle in the distance. As you walk in that direction, the sound of drumming gets louder, yet when you arrive there, you see no drums, no people. Not even a cat. Something is pulling you into the circle, but you remember the cat-man's warning.

If you choose to step into the stone circle, turn to page 55.

If you reluctantly return to the cottage where Eleanor awaits, turn to page 90.

The big sea creature is bigger than your cottage, bigger than your cottage plus Wiets's and three others put together! It's a glossy black mass, and then you see its eye. Soon, water is spouting from its head, drenching the three of you, but you can't stop laughing.

"That," says Kees, "is a whale!" You watch in wonder as the whale dives under and comes back up alongside the ship. It's not a unicorn, but it's certainly amazing!

You and Wiets look at each other, and at that moment, you know you are never going back to your village. There's a wide world out there full of creatures you never imagined you'd ever see, and you want to see all of it!

You and Wiets get work on ships traveling up and down the North Sea. You stop in Scotland many times, as well as Amsterdam, and many other places. You never see a real unicorn again, but your travels bring endless fascination. You love your life of adventure!

The End

Back in the cottage, the sound of drumming fades. You climb back into the nest of blankets, and this time, it's easy to sleep.

When you wake up, Eleanor is curled by your chest, but there's a second white cat beside her.

"Good morning," you say, looking around for your host. The second cat perks up.

"Where did you come from?" you ask the cat. It flicks its tail.

You make some tea and find some dried fish in the cupboard to eat. You share some with the cats. Remembering the milk you had for dinner, you go outside to see if there's a cow nearby.

It's a damp morning, and too misty for you to see the stone circle. You stroll around, looking for a cow, and you spot one resting in the meadow. The closer you get, the less it looks like a cow and more like a . . . unicorn!

But there's no horn! The poor unicorn is bleeding from a wound on top of its head.

You rush over and wrap your arms around its neck. Unicorn blood trickles onto your arm. You've heard of people cutting off unicorn horns, and right now, that seems like the cruelest thing you can imagine.

Go on to the next page.

You know a bit about healing from Marie-Claire, the herbalist in your village. You need something to stop the bleeding. You examine the grasses until you find a spider web stretched between some thistles. As carefully as you can, you lift the web off the thistles and place it over the unicorn's wound.

The bleeding stops, and the unicorn nuzzles you. As gently as you can, you guide the unicorn back to the cottage, hoping it isn't scared of cats.

Inside, the two cats are napping, but they leap up as soon as the unicorn enters. Luckily, the unicorn pays no attention to their excited antics. You settle the unicorn by the fire. Even though you're hungry, all you want to do is lie next to the unicorn and stroke its head.

Turn to the next page.

However, Eleanor has other ideas! She stands by the door, meowing urgently.

"You want to go outside?" you ask as you open the door for her. Eleanor steps through the door and looks back at you expectantly. She meows again and flicks her tail.

You look back at the unicorn. It seems to have fallen asleep, and the second cat is snoozing beside it.

"Okay," you say, and follow Eleanor. She leads you to a small pond, and you see where the fish from the cupboard come from. But Eleanor isn't looking for fish. She paws at a strange bluish moss growing on rocks at the edge of the pond. You scrape some up and hold it to your face. The cat meows sharply.

Turn to page 99.

You look at the red-capped goblin, now just a few feet away. You take a deep breath, and jump down from the wall onto the rock pile.

The next thing you feel is such overwhelming pain that you can't even think. It hurts too much to breathe or moan. You lie there on the stones, waiting for death.

You have no idea how much time has passed before you feel something wet on your cheek. Tears? Blood? You open one eye to a milky glow. It takes all your strength, but you blink both eyes open. There's a unicorn leaning over you, licking your cheek. The last thing you do is smile.

The End

You race down a hallway and out of the castle, running faster than you ever thought possible! You don't even turn to see if you are being followed. The forest looks frightening, but you need a place to hide. You wander a while between the trees, and finally find a large boulder to sleep beside. You are breathing so hard that at first, it's hard to fall asleep, but eventually, exhaustion overwhelms you.

It's still nighttime when you open your eyes. You struggle for a moment to remember where you are, and look around to remind yourself. You can't see much except a pair of green catlike eyes watching you!

Go on to the next page.

You blink, and the green eyes do, too. As your eyes get used to the darkness, you can make out the shape of a large black cat with a white patch on its chest. Even though this cat is the biggest you've ever seen—about the size of a large dog—it's still just a cat, and you've always liked cats. It hasn't attacked you yet, so maybe you should try to make friends with it.

Then you remember the frightening footsteps in the castle. Could this cat be what you heard?

If you call the cat over, turn to page 120.

If you run from the cat, turn to page 124.

The stone steps are very uneven, so you can't exactly run up them, but as quickly and quietly as you can, you hurry up to a landing. At the top, you peer down at the creature that enters the hall, and your heart stops.

Even in the darkness of twilight, you can see a red pointy cap!

It looks like some kind of goblin, not any taller than you, but much hairier. He's wearing boots made of iron and is carrying a spiked club. You squint your eyes to see better. Is he trailing blood?

You don't dare take a step, or even breathe.

Turn to page 98.

He turns around slowly, sniffing the air. Then he starts coming up the stairs. Each time his metal boots hit a stone step, you feel your death approach.

You turn to run, but realize that the second floor is mostly in ruins and open to the sky. There's no place to hide! You glance back at the goblin. He's just two steps from the top.

You scramble to the top of a broken wall and look down at the ground below. It's not terribly far to jump, but you would land on a pile of rocks.

If you decide to jump, turn to page 93.

If you are afraid to jump, turn to page 100.

She turns and starts heading back to the cottage. You follow her back, carrying the moss.

Inside the cottage, Eleanor rubs the unicorn's head with her tail and looks at you expectantly. As you put the moss on the unicorn's wound, both cats start purring loudly. The unicorn lifts its head with renewed energy.

You decide to go back to the pond to get more moss and try to catch a fish for breakfast. When you return, you examine the unicorn's head and are amazed to see a little nub of horn has grown back!

You spend a few more days at the cottage, nursing the unicorn while its horn grows back. The cat-man never returns, and the cottage becomes home for you, the two cats, and your unicorn. Every morning, Eleanor leads you to something new—a patch of berries, an ancient apple tree, and one day, a lost and lonely cow.

As the unicorn regains its strength, winter approaches. It really seems better not to travel in the cold, especially when the cottage is so inviting. You spend the winter, and then the rainy spring, with the unicorn, the two magical cats, and a cow. The seasons pass. You have a home, and a unicorn.

The End

100

The red-capped goblin reaches the landing and raises his iron club.

You take a huge breath, open your mouth, and scream as fiercely as you can. The goblin drops the club and covers his ears.

You take a second breath and discover you can scream even louder. You grab the club and now you're in charge!

"Go!" you shout, pointing down the steps. You swing the club up to your shoulder.

The goblin turns and scurries down the steps, but on the way, he trips. As he tumbles to the bottom, his iron boots make a terrible sound.

This is your chance to escape. You dash down the steps.

At the bottom, you take one quick look at the crumpled body, then run out of the castle.

Go on to the next page.

You feel nervous being outdoors at night, but at least you have the iron club for protection. You feel too jittery to sleep, so you decide to make your way as best you can in the moonlight. In case that goblin isn't dead, you want to get far away from the castle.

You walk through the night. As the sun starts to rise, you think about your terrifying encounter with the goblin and the red-haired woman's warning about Redcap. Why didn't you listen? You decide to go back to get more advice from the woman in the red dress.

Turn to the next page.

Nothing looks familiar as you walk back to town. Just when you feel you must be going in the wrong direction, a white cat appears beside you. This cat is clean and cared for. It must live in a house. If you follow the cat, maybe it will lead you there.

The cat leads you through a lush green valley and along a river where you stop to drink. After a few hours, you arrive in a town, but you can't remember if it's Edinburgh until you see the sign with the winged unicorn.

You knock on the door. When the red-haired woman sees you again, she smiles and takes your hand.

"I'm back," you announce. "Something terrifying happened."

The red-haired woman nods and picks up the cat. "That's why I suggested you take Eleanor. I sent her to find you. Wandering around Scotland on your own is really dangerous."

"I know that now! I think I might just want to go home."

The woman strokes the cat, then says, "I offered you a job before, and that offer still stands, if you want it. But if you really want to go home, I can take you to the harbor and help you get on the right boat."

If you accept the job, turn to page 70.

If you say you just want to go home, turn to page 128.

"I worried so much when you did not return from saying goodbye to Wiets!" she exclaims. "What took you so long?"

It takes a while to tell her about the unicorn you saw being loaded on a ship, falling off another boat, getting rescued and reunited with Wiets, and ending up in Scotland at a castle with another unicorn.

"Let me guess," says Marie-Claire. "You turned that unicorn into a cat."

"Exactly, but you know I never mastered reversing that spell. Can you do it?"

"Of course," Marie-Claire says, "but let's do it outside. I don't want a unicorn in my house."

Undoing the spell involves saying it backward and also doing all the hand movements in reverse. As Marie-Claire performs it, you watch the cat transform into a unicorn.

It stands there proudly, with green eyes flashing and horn glowing. You throw your arms around the unicorn's neck.

"There's something odd about this unicorn," says Marie-Claire as she turns the unicorn's head this way and that for a closer look. "The eyes, certainly, but there's something else...."

You're not listening. You're making plans for your new life with a unicorn!

The End

You hurl yourself on the man and bite his ear. He shrieks and flings you off. Before you can scramble to your feet, someone pushes you down and smacks your face. Someone is now sitting on you and yelling! So many people are brawling that you can't even see Wiets anymore. You close your eyes and wish you were somewhere else.

The man sitting on you is abruptly pushed off and someone yanks you to your feet. "I was trying to defend my friend," you cry, but of course, no one understands. A stout woman grabs your hair and pulls you over to the stocks.

You already know what will happen. You are pushed to the ground and your feet placed in holes in a wooden frame so you can't move. While you try to protest, someone drags Wiets over and his feet are shoved in the holes next to your feet. You can't stand, never mind walk away.

The abuse continues. People yell and throw rotten food at you.

"When we get out of this, let's just go home," you tell Wiets. "I don't care about the unicorn anymore."

"Agreed! We're on the first boat back to Bruges," he says.

After two miserable days and nights in the stocks, you and Wiets are released. You know the way back to Edinburgh, and have just enough money from Wiets's wages to pay for a voyage home. Your days of travel are over!

The End

106

You run inside the castle shouting, "Help! Help!" You are so upset that you forget you are speaking Flemish and the Scots won't understand you.

A well-dressed young man grabs your arm and says, "What's wrong?"

He understands your language!

"My friend is hurt!"

The man immediately stops the fight, and helps Wiets to his feet. "I'm sorry," he says, "they are very drunk. This is not the way to treat foreign guests. Come inside and get cleaned up."

As you follow him back inside the castle, you ask, "How do you know Flemish?"

Go on to the next page.

"I had a tutor from Flanders. I'm happy to be able to practice it again."

He introduces himself as Eoin, and has the servants give you pitchers of warm water to wash with. He even hands you clean clothing.

Later, over bowls of soup, Eoin asks, "What brought you here?"

"We're looking for a unicorn that was taken from Flanders," you explain. "Do you know anything about that?"

Eoin shakes his head. "Not at all. We have a unicorn, but we've had it for years. My father caught it not far from here. I don't know why anyone would bother to bring a unicorn from Flanders when we have plenty here already."

Turn to the next page.

"Can we see the unicorn?" Wiets asks.

"Of course," Eoin replies, "but maybe tomorrow. Let the celebration in the courtyard wind down. You two must be exhausted."

Eoin leads you to rooms that are nothing like you have ever slept in before. There are tall windows and a polished wooden floor. The bed is high off the ground and surrounded by curtains. The bed linens smell fresh and there's a sprig of lavender on the pillow. You feel like royalty curling up in that bed!

In the morning, a servant brings you a tray of food. Breakfast in bed!

A little later, Eoin knocks on the door. "Would you like to see our unicorn?"

Turn to page 110.

It's been hours since your breakfast with the fairies, so you decide to see if you can get some food inside the castle. You knock, and then knock again. Finally, you push open the door.

The castle is splendidly decorated with tapestries and leather-bound chests. "Hello!" you call, but no one answers.

You wander into a hallway lined with paintings and stop. The first painting shows a unicorn standing beside a magnificently dressed woman with jewels adorning her wrist. The crazy thing is, the woman looks exactly like your mother, except that your mother never had any nice clothing, never mind jewelry! You blink your eyes and look again. Is your memory playing tricks on you?

It's too much to think about, so you walk over to the next painting, only to find it's your father, wearing a clean linen shirt and a silk vest. Next to him is a dog, and with a shock, you realize it's the dog you had when you were younger!

You feel you might faint. You sit down on a trunk to think, but there is no way to make any sense of this! When you push yourself up from the trunk, you hear a dull clinking sound. Opening the trunk, you find it is halfway full with gold coins. You pick one up to examine it. There'a unicorn on it!

At that moment, you remember the fairies giving you luck, and realize you received not just good luck, but wonderful luck, and a whole new life!

The End

110

You and Wiets follow him outside to the garden. There, in the center, is a beautifully fashioned iron cage with a unicorn inside. It tosses its head as you approach. You notice it has green eyes, not something you have ever seen on a unicorn before.

"Do you ever ride this unicorn?" you ask Eoin.

"No," he answers. "I don't believe I've ever seen the unicorn outside this cage." You notice the large padlock.

"That seems sad," you say.

Eoin shrugs. "It's a unicorn. It's just for decoration. Come, let's go inside. I'd like you to teach me some more Flemish."

Go on to the next page.

That night, you slip into Wiets's room.

"I want to free that unicorn," you tell him.

"Well, I don't," says Wiets, rolling over in bed. "I like it here. The food is great, and I love this bed. Eoin seems really nice. If the hardest work I have to do is teach him Flemish, I'm in heaven."

"But that poor unicorn locked in the cage!" you remind him.

"Do you remember the drought of 1507 when we had no water? Do you remember the winter the whole village ran out of food? Do you remember what it's like to have to plow without a horse? I'm staying here as long as Eoin will have us."

"Everything you say is true, but a unicorn shouldn't be locked in a cage," you insist.

"I can't believe you're even thinking about stealing Eoin's unicorn! It's one thing to rescue the one that was taken from Flanders, but this is a Scottish unicorn that belongs to him. You've got no right to steal it!"

If you agree with Wiets, turn to the next page.

If you decide to rescue the unicorn on your own, turn to page 114.

"You're right," you tell Wiets. "Sleep well. I'll see you in the morning."

Breakfast the next morning is even better than the day before. You spend the morning speaking Flemish with Eoin and Wiets, and the afternoon sitting by the green-eyed unicorn. Dinner is abundant, and you finally meet Eoin's father, but he doesn't speak Flemish, so there's not much you can say except thank you. You decide to learn Scottish.

The days pass, and then the months. It's just a few years later that you end up marrying a member of Eoin's family. For your wedding present, the unicorn is set free.

The End

114

"I'll think about it," you tell Wiets, but your mind is already made up.

Rather than going back to bed, you sneak outside to the unicorn. Its eyes are closed and it's purring like a cat! You've never known a unicorn to purr like that, and then you start to think—weren't those green eyes a little catlike?

You remember a spell Marie-Claire, the healer in your village, taught you years ago for turning things into cats.

You smile, thinking back to the rabbit you transformed into a cat, and how mad your father was when you turned your dog into a cat. You never learned how to change cats back to their original form, but Marie-Claire could, so you got your dog back eventually.

If you could turn the unicorn into a cat, it could slip between the bars of the cage very easily. In fact, it would be much easier to take a cat back to Flanders than a unicorn.

Go on to the next page.

It takes you a while to remember the spell. You reach your hands into the cage and rest one on the unicorn's head, then close your eyes afterward and say:

"You hear all and purr.
In darkness you see.
You're covered with fur.
As a cat, come to me."

What's tricky is that there are certain finger movements you have to make with your other hand, one movement for each word, and you hope you remember them correctly.

Turn to the next page.

116

Even before you open your eyes, you feel the unicorn shrinking and its fur growing longer. When you feel certain the magic has worked, you open your eyes. A white cat stands up and walks between the bars of the cage right into your hands.

You scoop up the cat and make your way past the castle walls. You're sad to leave Wiets without saying goodbye, but pretty pleased with yourself for remembering Marie-Claire's spell.

After a while, you get tired of carrying the cat and wonder if it would follow you. When you put it down, it scampers ahead, staying on the path back to Edinburgh.

You pass the walls of the city just as the sun is rising. You are still following the cat when it stops by a house with a winged unicorn sign. The cat sits by the door and meows. You are eager to get to the harbor and find a boat back to Bruges, but that sign is pulling you to it.

If you pick up the cat and continue on to the harbor, go on to the next page.

If you knock on the door, turn to page 118.

Finding the harbor is easy enough, but you don't have any money to pay for a voyage. You must find a job.

The only captain who is willing to hire you is first stopping at several places in England on the way to Flanders. It's a longer journey than you would have liked, but the days at sea pass quickly.

You start to really like the cat. It playfully bats at your nose, and at night, sleeps curled up by your chest. The cat catches mice that scurry around the boat, which pleases the crew so much that they give you both extra fish to eat.

As soon as you get back to your village, you visit Marie-Claire. She's delighted to see you!

Turn to page 103.

118

You pick up the cat and knock on the door. The woman who answers it is dazzling! Her hair is red, her tunic is red, and you can't remember when you last saw such brightness. Also, it seems like there are small silver stars in her hair.

She takes one look at the cat and exclaims, "Mikayla!"

The cat leaps into her arms. She says something to you, but you can't understand until she takes your hand. Then she says in Flemish, "I turned this cat into a unicorn many years ago. I don't know how she ended up as a cat again!"

"I turned the unicorn into a cat," you tell her proudly.

"Did you?" She raises her eyebrows, and you can tell you've impressed her.

"Yes, I wanted to get the unicorn out of a cage, and the only way I could think to do that was to make it into a cat."

"Nice work!" exclaims the woman. "You were right to free a unicorn. But tell me, how did you learn this magic?"

Turn to page 129.

Finally, the cat stops and looks back at you, flicking her tail. Straight ahead is a unicorn!

The unicorn is nibbling moss growing on the side of a tree. It pauses and gazes at you calmly. Your heart beats with excitement as you realize there is at least one unicorn left in Flanders after all!

Every day from then on, Anaya leads you to a unicorn. Sometimes there are two unicorns, and sometimes a baby too! You realize the red-haired woman sent you home with a cat that can hunt unicorns, and that's how you spend your days.

The End

120

"Come here, kitty," you whisper, motioning with your hand.

The cat saunters over and curls up next to you. You stroke its head, and it starts to purr. Before long, the cat is nestled in your lap, keeping you warm.

"Where do you live, kitty?" you ask. "You must be eating well to get this big!"

The cat meows in response, and to your astonishment, you understand it saying, "My name is Sith, and I live alone because everyone is afraid of me. People either try to kill me or they run away from me. I'm so lonely!"

"Oh, Sith," you say, "that's so sad! We can stay together. I'm trying to find a unicorn, and maybe you can help."

No sooner are the words out of your mouth than Sith leaps off your lap and into the darkness. You wonder what you said wrong. Suddenly, you feel lonely too!

Go on to the next page.

You have just about given up hope of ever seeing Sith again when the cat returns, dragging a unicorn by the neck!

"What?" you shout. "Let go of that unicorn!"

"I was only trying to help," Sith meows, sheepishly.

"Well, thanks, but a dead unicorn does not help me!"

"It's not dead yet," Sith meows. The cat nudges the bleeding unicorn with a paw, and you can see it is still alive. The unicorn's eyes flutter open. You wipe the blood with the hem of your tunic.

"I need a safe place for this poor unicorn to recover," you tell Sith, "and it's not going to be in that castle."

"Of course not," meows Sith. "The evil goblin Redcap lives in this castle. Even I don't go there! I know a cave that's big enough for the three of us. Follow me."

Turn to the next page.

122

It's not easy to drag the injured unicorn to the cave, and you fight back tears each time you hear it whimper. By the time you get there, the unicorn's coat is covered with dirt and leaves. Once the unicorn is settled, you go off to find a spider web to put over the wound. It's a trick you learned from Marie-Claire, an herbalist from your village.

At first, the unicorn is understandably terrified of Sith, but slowly gets used to Sith curling up nearby. Sith becomes very useful, carrying back in its mouth fresh moss for the unicorn, and a small red squirrel for you to cook. You're not used to starting a fire by rubbing rocks together, so it takes you many tries, but eventually, you manage to roast the squirrel. You are hungry enough that it tastes delicious!

By the time the unicorn has healed completely, you've gotten pretty comfortable living in the cave with Sith. You expected the unicorn to leave when it was well enough, but it turns out the unicorn is very comfortable too! The three of you spend your days roaming the forest and your nights curled up together in the cozy cave.

The End

124

You scramble to your feet and run away. It's nearly impossible to see in the dark forest, so you've barely gone ten feet when you trip on something and land face first on the ground. A second later, the cat is on your back, sinking its teeth into your neck.

The End

"Stop! Stop!" you shout, but the unicorn continues straight toward the edge above the waterfall. You squeeze your eyes shut and hold your breath as you feel yourself plunging into the air.

You land at the base of the waterfall with an enormous splash. You are both drenched, but still alive!

You are still shaking wet hair out of your face when the unicorn starts running again. Glancing back, you see the men and dogs clamoring above the waterfall. It doesn't look like they will give up the chase so easily. You are going to need a place to hide.

In the distance, you see what looks like a huge pile of stones. You steer the unicorn out of the river and toward the fallen stones of what you now see is a once-grand castle. You climb down and lead the unicorn inside. The roof has long since collapsed, but you can make out where rooms and hallways once stood.

Turn to the next page.

126

Suddenly, you notice the birds! The place is filled with long-legged white birds, sort of like herons, but not exactly. They are preening their feathers, pecking the ground, and sipping from puddles, completely unconcerned by your arrival.

You hear barking as the dogs approach. The birds freeze, then start flapping their wings furiously. They tilt their heads toward the sky and make scary screeching cries. Strangely, the birds don't fly. They just continue to beat their wings and screech.

You climb on the remains of a wall to see what is happening outside. The dogs have stopped running and are cowering. The men are covering their ears with their hands and the horses are neighing nervously.

When you look back, you see that small wings are emerging from the unicorn's back! You climb on the unicorn, watching in amazement as its wings grow larger. The birds are still squawking when you start to fly, but then in one great swoosh of flapping feathers, the birds are soaring around you!

You look down on the ruins, the glistening river, and farther away, the castle where you spent the night. You feel momentarily dizzy, but then know what to do. You locate the sun in the eastern sky and turn to the south. It may take a while, but you and the unicorn are flying home to Flanders.

The End

"Thank you," you say. "I just want to go home. I think I have enough money to pay for passage back to Bruges."

"This time, you really must take a cat," she insists. She looks around at the several white cats that have now gathered around her. "Not Eleanor. Here, you can take Anaya." She picks up the smallest of the cats and hands it to you.

"All right," you say with uncertainty. You nuzzle the little white cat and wonder why exactly the woman thinks you will need it back home. The cat blinks its green eyes sleepily and purrs. "Can you show me how to get to the harbor?"

The red-haired woman leads you to the harbor and negotiates for you and the little cat to sail on a boat leaving later that day.

You spend most of the voyage home curled up in a nest of blankets with Anaya in your arms. You keep thinking back to the terrifying goblin who almost killed you. You also think of your friend Wiets, who won't be there when you return. Anaya is the only thing that cheers you up.

Back in your village, your heart is heavy with disappointment. You put down the cat to open the door to your cottage. As soon as Anaya's paws touch the earth, she scampers off into the nearby woods.

You run after her calling, "Anaya!" Why did the red-haired woman have to give you this mischievous cat? You trail Anaya between trees and over rocks, skirting a muddy puddle. You can't keep up with her!

Turn to page 119.

You tell her all about the many things you've learned from Marie-Claire.

"I could use a skilled assistant," she says. "Most of my work involves turning cats into unicorns, but I have some other plans as well."

"Winged unicorns?" you ask.

"Exactly! Would you like a job?"

"That's exciting, and I'm really tempted," you admit to her, "but I was hoping to bring the cat to Flanders and have Marie-Claire turn it back to a unicorn."

"I'm sorry," she replies. "Mikayla isn't going anywhere after all those years in a cage. She's probably sick of being a unicorn after that." She runs her fingers though her hair and a few silver stars fly off. "Please stay. I really could use some help here."

You catch one of the stars in your hand and answer, "I will!"

The End

130

You follow the fairy to a narrow path behind the waterfall, and into a cave. You expect it to be completely dark, but there is an odd bluish glow that makes it possible for you to see a little bit. There are several other fairies there, and they cluster around you, patting your arms and shoulders very gently.

They offer you a plate of something fluffy and blue. At first, you do not eat it.

It doesn't look like food, and it could be a dangerous potion. Yet as time passes, you become famished. The fairies seem really kind.

You take just a tiny nibble. It is sweet and fresh and utterly delicious! You fill your mouth with more. You haven't tasted anything this sweet since you ate wild berries back home, and nothing you've eaten since leaving Bruges has been even half this good. You sigh with pleasure and then eat more.

When you are finally full, you curl up with the fairies. They drape their arms around you to keep you warm. To your surprise, it feels very cozy, and you quickly fall asleep.

The next morning, you enjoy some more blue fluff for breakfast. You're having a wonderful time with the fairies, but you do have a unicorn to find, so you sing your story to the fairies and ask if they can help you.

All eight of the fairies nod their heads yes. Singing in unison, they explain that they can give you luck, but the catch is, they can't control whether it's good luck or bad luck, so it's risky.

Turn to page 133.

132

You politely decline the fairy's hospitality and walk away. Almost immediately, the weather turns foggy, so you can't follow the sun. You look back, but can't see even six feet behind you. There's no point wandering in this mist, so you climb onto a big rock and close your eyes. It's not comfortable, yet you fall asleep very easily.

When you wake up, you find yourself in your own bed, in your own cottage in Flanders. You pull your hands out of the covers to rub your eyes and discover you are clutching the unicorn-embroidered handkerchief, the one you gave Wiets. Or did you?

The End

"Please give me good luck," you sing.

The fairies huddle together with their arms around each other's shoulders. They begin singing in strange tones, low like bullfrogs and high like bird whistles, echoing around the fairy circle.

Suddenly, they all throw their arms up and burst out laughing!

The fairies lead you out of the cave to where a gray horse stands waiting. You climb on its back, and wave goodbye to the fairies, and the horse trots away. Even though you don't know where you're going, the horse seems to, so you just hold on to the mane and ride.

After a few hours, you arrive at a castle, and waiting by the door is a unicorn! You can't be sure it's the unicorn from Flanders, but you hug it anyway. The unicorn licks your cheek affectionately.

Turn to page 109.

ABOUT THE ARTISTS

Illustrator: Suzanne Nugent received her BFA in illustration from Moore College of Art & Design in Philadelphia, Pennsylvania. She now resides with her husband, Fred, in Philadelphia and works as a freelance illustrator. She first discovered her love for *Choose Your Own Adventure*® books when she was only four years old, which inspired her to become an artist.

Cover Artist: Marco Cannella was born in Ascoli Piceno, Italy, on September 29, 1972. Marco started his career in art as a decorator and an illustrator when he was a college student. He became a full-time professional in 2001 when he received the flag-prize for the "Palio della Quintana" (one of the most important Italian historical games). Since then, he has worked as an illustrator at Studio Inventario in Bologna. He has also been a scenery designer for professional theater companies. He works for the production company ASP srl in Rome as a character designer and set designer on the preproduction of a CG feature film. In 2004 he moved to Bangalore, India, to serve as full-time art director on this project.

ABOUT THE AUTHOR

Deborah Lerme Goodman grew up in New York, where she saw The Hunt of the Unicorn tapestries that inspired a lifetime's fascination. Those amazing textiles also inspired her to study tapestry weaving in college! Besides *The Rescue of the Unicorn* and *The Magic of the Unicorn*, she has written three other books in the original *Choose Your Own Adventure* series. She lives with her husband in Cambridge, Massachusetts, where she teaches English to adult immigrants.

For games, activities, and other fun stuff,
or to write to Deborah Lerme Goodman,
visit us online at CYOA.com

THE RESCUE OF
THE UNICORN

This book is different from other books.

You and YOU ALONE are in charge of what happens in this story.

There are dangers, choices, adventures, and consequences. YOU must use all of your numerous talents and much of your enormous intelligence. The wrong decision could end in disaster—even death. But don't despair. At any time, YOU can go back and make another choice, alter the path of your story, and change its result.

You have left your small village behind for new things. In the crowded port of Bruges, many chances for a new life await you. But when you stand before the giant ships, you see a caged unicorn. You know that's not right. Is the unicorn headed for a new life as well? YOU and YOU alone are capable of following this magical beast, and saving its life!